Ali's Amazing Adventures In Dubai

by
JANEEN TEDFORD

Illustrated by
EMMA STUART

For my little one, Stephanie, a true gift from God. You fill my life with joy and I love you so very much. Special thanks to my husband, Michael for all your support and for believing in me.

ISBN : 978-1-79398-287-2

Target Audience: For children.
Subjects: Animals – Juvenile Fiction.

This book belongs to.

· ·

Ali shivered as he woke and found himself alone in the desert. The big truck had gone, along with his mother and the other horses. He stood up with a fright and looked at the long road in front of him.

As he began to walk along the road, he heard a voice coming from the sand. Looking down, he saw a strange animal that had no legs. "Who are you? What are you?" asked Ali.

"I'm Saeed and I'm a snake," replied the strange animal. "I live under the sand to avoid the heat."

"Hello," said Ali. He told Saeed that a big truck he and his mother were on had left him behind in the desert. "I must find my mother," he said sadly.

"Well, I will help you find her!" replied Saeed.

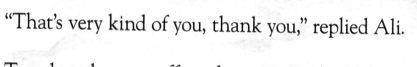

"That's very kind of you, thank you," replied Ali.

Together they set off as the sun streaked beautiful colours of pink and orange across the desert sky.

After a while, Ali and Saeed saw large brown animals walking towards them. They had long legs, very long necks, and big bumps on their backs! One of these animals walked up to Ali and Saeed.

"Hello," he said. "I'm Khalid the camel."

Ali and Saeed told Khalid about
their journey to find Ali's mother.
Khalid said he would like to help them but first
they all needed to stop for a drink of water.

Khalid led Ali and Saeed to an oasis in the desert.

After drinking some water and having a rest beneath the big, beautiful trees, Ali and his friends set off on their journey once more.

Soon Ali saw an unusual animal walking over the sand dunes. It was white and had two big black things sticking out of its head! Scared, Ali jumped behind Khalid.

"Hello, I'm Omar the Oryx," said the animal.

"What are those strange things on your head?" asked Ali nervously.

"These are my horns!" laughed Omar.

Ali told Omar that he, Saeed and Khalid were on a journey to find his mother.

"Then I will come, too!" said Omar.

Not too long afterwards, they saw a busy road ahead.

"Oh, no! How are we going to cross this?" sighed Ali.

"You need to cross it very carefully – and make sure you don't get hurt!"

The small voice came from a big ball of spikes on the sand.

"Who are you? asked Ali.

"I'm Hakim, and I'm a hedgehog," the ball of spikes replied.

After Ali explained his journey to find his mother, Hakim laughed. "Then I must show you how to cross this busy road first." He led them to a pedestrian crossing and said, "This is the safe way to get to the other side."

On the other side of the road, Ali heard a swooping sound above them. "Hello! I am Farhad the falcon!" he called out.

Ali explained he was on a journey with his friends to find his mother.

Farhad replied, "I will fly ahead and see if I can find her for you."

And so they all set off again to search for Ali's mother.

In a while, Ali and his friends found themselves in a big city. There were plenty of tall, colourful buildings, and countless cars and people passing all around them. "We're in Dubai," exclaimed Farhad excitedly.

Ali looked around, and in front of him saw an extremely big building shaped like a ship's sail. "That is the Burj Al Arab, the tallest hotel in the world," said Farhad. "I've flown over it many times to chase the pigeons away."

Ali saw an unusual place near the Burj Al Arab where people were playing in water. "That's Wild Wadi!" came a voice from above. "It's where people go and play and have lots of fun on different water rides."

Ali looked up and saw a large white bird hovering nearby. "I am Samira and I'm a seagull," the bird shouted down.

Ali told Samira about his journey with his friends to find his mother.

"I will try to help you," replied Samira.

But first, Ali and his friends went into Wild Wadi and began to play and have fun in the water. They had a tremendous time on all the different types of water rides.

After a while they decided to continue on their journey. In the distance they spotted an oddly shaped building. "That is Ski Dubai," said Samira.

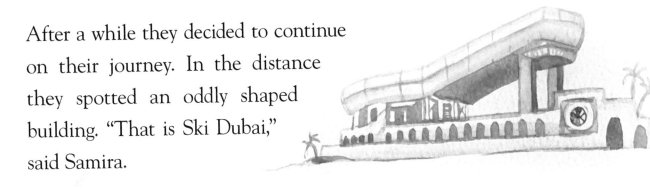

They all entered the Mall of The Emirates to have a look at this strange place. There were lots of children playing in a white powder that Samira said was called snow. Ali and his friends decided to join them.

They had so much fun in the cold snow — but soon they needed to carry on their journey.

Next they saw a very tall building sparkling in the distance. "And what is that?" asked Ali.

"That is the Burj Khalifa," said Khalid. "It's the tallest building in the world."

They all decided to have a closer look at the big, shiny building. It was very tall indeed, and the glass sparkled in the sunlight, like silver.

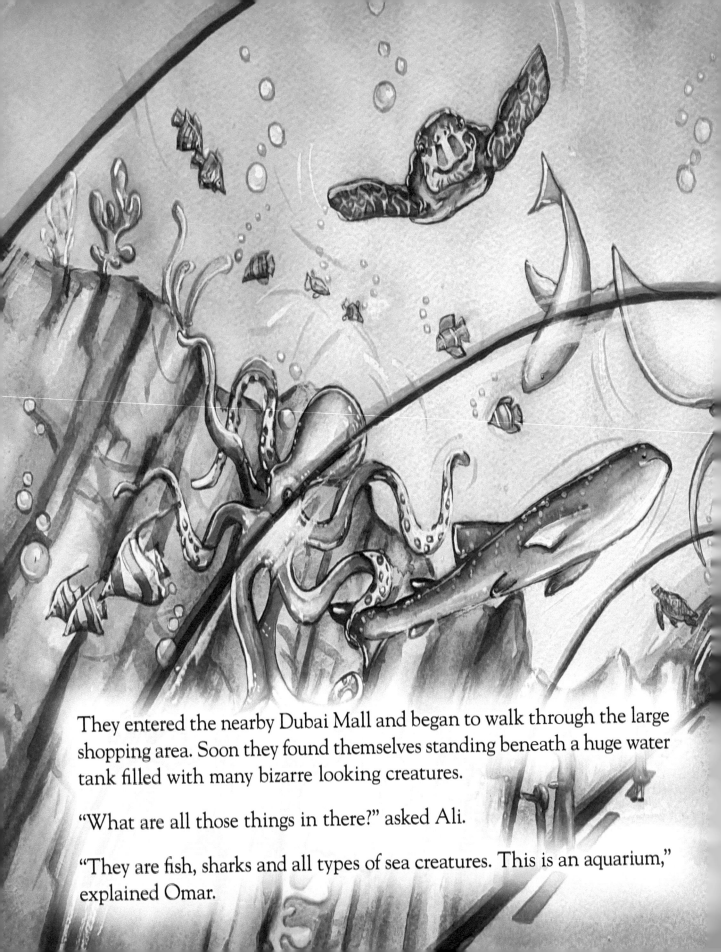

They entered the nearby Dubai Mall and began to walk through the large shopping area. Soon they found themselves standing beneath a huge water tank filled with many bizarre looking creatures.

"What are all those things in there?" asked Ali.

"They are fish, sharks and all types of sea creatures. This is an aquarium," explained Omar.

They all stood below the large aquarium and looked up in wonder at all the different types of fish and sharks. They could not believe how many creatures were all in one place.

"This is incredible," said Ali, "but we must continue our journey. I need to find my mother."

As they set off once more, Farhad swooped out of the sky. "I think I know where your mother is Ali!" he announced. "She may be at Meydan, where the Dubai World Cup is being held."

So they followed Farhad in search of Ali's mother.

Before long they came across a small lake, and there in the water were remarkable tall pink birds with big beaks. They were all standing with their heads in the water!

"What are these strange birds?" asked Ali, just as one of them looked up towards him …

"Hello! My name is Fatima and I'm a flamingo!" she said.

Ali explained to Fatima that he was in search of his mother and introduced all his new friends to her.

Not long after leaving Fatima, they all reached Meydan. Ali was amazed at the size and beauty of all he saw. As he looked around, he heard a voice in the distance shout his name. "Ali, oh my son, you're safe!"

It was Ali's mother, and she came running up to greet him. Ali was so excited to see her and told her about his amazing journey and how his new friends had helped him find her.

Ali's mother thanked them all. She was so grateful that they had taken such great care of Ali and helped him travel through the desert safely and through the great city of Dubai to find her.

THE END

CPSIA information can be obtained
at www.ICGtesting.com
Printed in the USA
LVHW071219071019
633399LV00004B/504/P